X

Cat Among the Pigeons

Also by Kit Wright
Hot Dog and Other Poems

Chosen by Kit Wright
Poems for 9-year-olds and Under
Poems for Over 10-year-olds

CAT

Among
the Pigeons

Poems by Kit Wright

Illustrated by Posy Simmonds

VIKING KESTREL

VIKING KESTREL
Penguin Books Ltd, 27 Wrights Lane, London W8 5TZ (Publishing and Editorial)
and Harmondsworth, Middlesex, England (Distribution and Warehouse)
Viking Penguin Inc., 40 West 23rd Street, New York, New York 10010, U.S.A.
Penguin Books Australia Ltd, Ringwood, Victoria, Australia
Penguin Books Canada Limited, 2801 John Street, Markham, Ontario, Canada L3R 1B4
Penguin Books (N.Z.) Ltd, 182-190 Wairau Road, Auckland 10, New Zealand

First published 1987

British Library Cataloguing in Publication Data
Wright, Kit
    Cat among the pigeons: poems.
    I. Title
    821'.914   PZ8.3

    ISBN 0-670-81711-2

Filmset in Plantin (Linotron 202) by
Rowland Phototypesetting Ltd, Bury St Edmunds, Suffolk

Printed in Great Britain by
Butler & Tanner Ltd, Frome and London

For Zoe Redmond, Zoe Hilton,
Zoe Newton, Alexander Wright,
Caroline Maclean, Spike Sterne,
Dominic Scriven, Timothy Scriven,
Finbar Wright and Charlotte Martin

Contents

Nothing Else

There's nothing I can't see
From here.

There's nothing I can't be
From here.

Because my eyes
Are open wide
To let the big
World come inside,

I think I can see me
From here.

A Simple Story of Accrington Stanley

A nasty old woman once lived in Accrington Town
With a face that was blocked with rage like a stopped
    clock,
And she spoke harsh words in a sort of a strangled
    voice,
Like a person who for some reason has swallowed a
    sock.

But mostly she said nothing at all. It was no good
Wishing that woman good morning or calling,
    'Goodnight',
But there was a boy in Accrington Town called Stanley
Who thought to himself he just might put things right.

He was kicking a football about on a waste-ground
    patch
By ragwort and chickweed against a garage wall,
And he spied a Coke can and widened the V-hole out
With a stone, and cut himself not too badly at all.

Then he stuffed the blazing ragwort and frosty
  chickweed
And mauvely smouldering willowherb into the can
And ran with it round to the nasty old woman of
  Accrington,
Who sat as lonely as an empty removal van.

Croaked, 'Why have you brought me this?' 'It's a
  present,' said Stanley.
'A present? Not ever has anyone brought me one.'
'Well, I have,' said Stanley. 'And so you have!' cried
  the lady,
And danced both up and down and shone like the sun.

Then she took his hands and jigged with him round
  the kitchen,
One foot up, then one and a half feet down,
And ever since then has been known as the jolliest
  woman
That ever pranced the streets of Accrington Town!

Well, an aeroplane would be good and an elephant
Is always acceptable, but they're hard to find,
And whatever you've got will do wonderfully well if
  you mean it;
Be kind to someone who's stuck. It makes them kind.

11

Charlotte's Dog

Daniel the spaniel has ears like rugs,
Teeth like prongs of electric plugs.

His back's a thundery winter sky,
Black clouds, white clouds rumbling by.

His nose is the rubber of an old squash ball
Bounced in the rain. His tail you'd call

A chopped-off rope with a motor inside
That keeps it walloping. Red-rimmed-eyed,

He whimpers like plimsolls on a wooden floor.
When he yawns he closes a crimson door.

When he barks it's a shark of a sound that bites
Through frosty mornings and icy nights.

When he sleeps he wheezes on a dozing lung:
Then he wakes you too with a wash of his tongue!

Round

Many hounds are found about
Bounding round the roundabout,
In and out the roundabout
And round and round the roundabout,

And when a hound *is* found about
Bounding round the roundabout,
We impound that bounding hound
And ground him in the downtown pound,

Where you for round about a pound
May reclaim your bounding hound,
But if you leave him in the pound
We'll hound him out of town!

Advice to Spiders

The spider is a very short person with very long legs
That are fine for advancing
On a fly in a sticky web
But utterly useless for dancing.

You can see two bees up
Over the sunny clover,
Body-popping,
But you can't imagine two spiders having a knees-up
On their springy floor.
It's those complicated legs that have stopped the
  bopping
For ever more.

They'd be so entangled
They'd get mangled,

So interrelated
They'd get amputated.

So I advise spiders:
Leave your dancing pumps on the shelf
And keep your legs to yourself.

Granny Tom

There's a cat among the pigeons
In the yard, in the yard,
And it seems he isn't trying
Very hard.
Should a pigeon chance to swoop,
You can see his whiskers droop
And his tail not twitch its loop
In the yard.

For the cat is growing old
In the yard, in the yard,
And the pigeons leave him cold.
He has starred
In his youth in many chases,
When he put them through their paces.
Now he knows just what his place is
In the yard.

He's a snoozer in the sun
And his hunting days are done.
He's a dozer by the wall
And he pounces not at all
For he knows he no more can. He
Might well be the pigeons' *granny*
In the yard!

Mothering

Half-falling, half-flying, the young sparrow
Looped from the nest, and the cat
Leaped and snagged it out of the air,
Padded into the shade
With the bird warm in her mouth,
Ripped it apart and ate it,
Then lay on her side in the kitchen
Among the feathers,
Suckling each one
Of her innocent kittens, and purring.

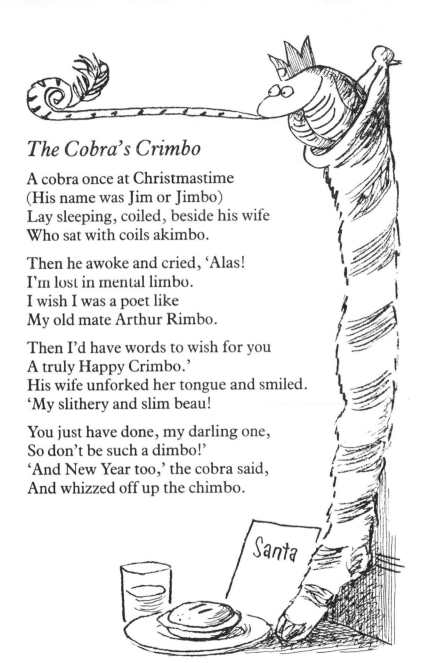

The Cobra's Crimbo

A cobra once at Christmastime
(His name was Jim or Jimbo)
Lay sleeping, coiled, beside his wife
Who sat with coils akimbo.

Then he awoke and cried, 'Alas!
I'm lost in mental limbo.
I wish I was a poet like
My old mate Arthur Rimbo.

Then I'd have words to wish for you
A truly Happy Crimbo.'
His wife unforked her tongue and smiled.
'My slithery and slim beau!

You just have done, my darling one,
So don't be such a dimbo!'
'And New Year too,' the cobra said,
And whizzed off up the chimbo.

Sadie Goes to Sea

A dinner lady
Whose name was Sadie
(Her boy called Roy
And her man called Stan)
In an old Land Rover
Went galloping over
The tussocky fields
Of the Isle of Man.

They met a squirrel
Whose name was Cyril
(Who came from the Wirral)
And gave him a lift:
They found a bonnet
With badges on it
And draped it over
That old gear-shift.

THE SEA

A water-logged welly
Name-marked 'Kelly'
They slung right on to
That rusty exhaust:
They picked up a rider
Who'd been astride a
Stallion but sadly
Got de-horsed.

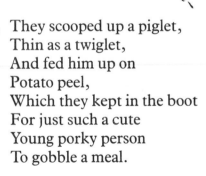

They scooped up a piglet,
Thin as a twiglet,
And fed him up on
Potato peel,
Which they kept in the boot
For just such a cute
Young porky person
To gobble a meal.

They found a donkey
Whose legs were wonky
And settled him down
In the back of the car:
They stole a rhino
With skin like lino,
Wrinkled and worn,
In a public bar.

Now, that old Land Rover
Was spilling over
With animal extras
And people too,
But it kept on bumping
All over the jumping
Fields of Man
With its personal zoo –

Till the dinner lady
Whose name was Sadie
Her boy called Roy
And her man called Stan,
The squirrel called Cyril
(Who came from the Wirral),
Mistreated, unseated,
The horse-riding man,

The twiglet piglet,
The wonky donkey,
The lino rhino
And all the rest
Jumped over a hedge
By the ocean's edge
And drove in shouting,
'WATER'S BEST!'

March Dusk

About the hour light wobbles
Between the day and night,

On paving-stones and cobbles
Rain hisses with weak spite

And plane trees dangling bobbles,
Drip leafless from numb height

Where wounded springtime hobbles
That soon will leap with light.

Fishing Vessel

The hawthorn tree
    that trawled its catch

of crimson berries
    in its scratchy net

a wild way out
    in the rending winds

dreams at anchor
    but soon will hoist

its new white sails
    on the late spring tide.

Sid the Rat

Sid was a rat
Who kept a hat shop,
Ordinary sort of stuff:

Pork pies,
Panamas,
Old flat caps,
Bowlers,
Boaters
For old fat chaps,
Deerstalkers,
Stetsons . . .
And that was *enough*
For *that* shop!

Yes, Sid was a rat
Who kept a hat shop,
Ordinary sort of trade:

Eels,
Elks,
Dirty old foxes,
Skinny
Kittens
In travelling boxes,
Elephants,
Owls . . .
And business *paid*
In *that* shop!

~ne day the Mayor knocked on the door,
'Sid, you can't stay here no more!
oing to knock your hat shop down
d a new road through the town!'

'Is that a fact?'
Said Sid the Rat,
'Is that a fact?'
Said he.
'We'll see!

You build your road and I'll get my hats,
And I'll stack them up like a block of flats

    Right in the middle
    And, hey-diddle-diddle,
    The cars won't know
    Which way to go!
    And I'll get the elk,
    And the dirty old fox,
    And the kitten
    Out of her travelling box,
    And the slithering eel,
    And the wise owl too,
    And the elephant
    On his way to the zoo,
    And I'll tell you what they'll do!

They'll pull those drivers out,
Willy-nilly,
And they'll tickle those drivers
And tickle them silly!
There'll be *huge* traffic jams
But they won't care!
So how do you like *that*,
Mr Mayor?'

'Oh,' said the Mayor.
'Oh dear,' said the Mayor.
'Hum,' said the Mayor.
'I fear,' said the Mayor,
'You'd better keep your hat shop, Sid,
And carry on the way you did!'

Sid

Did!

Dave Dirt's Jacket Pocket

In Dave's jacket pocket
the last time I looked
was half a cold burger
three days ago cooked,

a dead mouse, ten dog hairs,
a chip, chewing gum,
a two-week-old note
to the Head from his mum,

a very old conker
that mouldiness grows on,
a twisted Tube ticket
for blowing his nose on,

a bitten-off fingernail,
part of a snail,
the tongue of a snake
and a dry lizard's tail,

a piece of a sweet
just as sticky as glue,
all forming together
a horrible stew!

Don't ask him to show you.
Of this there's no doubt:
one look at the thing will
turn *you* inside out!

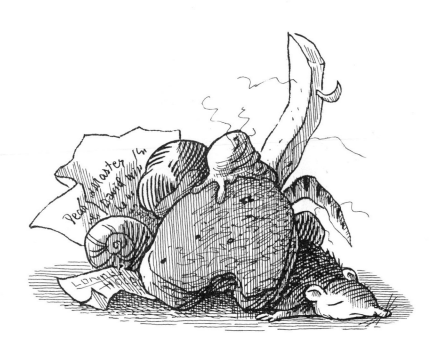

Get This Straight

Dear Uncle Sam, dear Uncle Sam,
Do you not *know* what sex I am,
Or is the whole thing just your little joke?

If it's a joke, I'm not amused
That you pretend to be confused:
It makes me yowl: it makes me boil and choke.

It's no good shouting, '*What* a chap!'
The fact is that I'm *not* a chap
And have no wish at all to be a bloke!

But there again, if your mistake
Is genuine – for heaven's sake,
Your head must truly be as thick as oak!

It's no good yelling, 'Attaboy!
Look lively! What's the matter, boy?'
The matter is that I am NOT A BLOKE!

Got that, Auntie?

Zoe's Ear-rings

She bought 'em in the autumn
After spotting 'em in Nottingham.
She took 'em home to Cookham
And she put 'em in a drawer

Till May came and the day came
When she wore 'em down to Shoreham,
But *nobody* was for 'em
So she wore 'em nevermore . . .

Till the wedding of her sister
To a mister out at Bicester,
Name of Jimmy, who said, '*Gimme*,'
So without 'em she went home,

But she nipped back down to nick 'em
For a knees-up in High Wycombe,
For an evening quite near Chevening
And a dawn at Kilmacolm.

They were in 'er for a dinner
Which was excellent, in Pinner,
And another one, a cracker,
In Majacca – that's in Spain –

Then she popped 'em on in Haddenham
And didn't feel too bad in 'em:
She felt in 'em, in Cheltenham,
Just as right as rain.

They looked smart on in Dumbarton,
They looked wizard on the Lizard,
They looked corking down in Dorking
And incredible in Crewe.

When she wore 'em into Rugely
They impressed the people hugely,
While in Fordham folk adored 'em,
And they *loved* 'em in West Looe!

The citizens of Kettering
Had never seen a better ring,
In fact no better pair of 'em –
'Take care of 'em!' they cried.

Then she slithered into Lytham with 'em,
Shaking out a rhythm with 'em,
Wobb-er-ling and jogg-er-ling
Her head from side to side.

Folk in Preston thought the best 'un
Was the right 'un. In New Brighton
And in Sefton, though, the *left* 'un
Was the one they favoured more,

While in Greenham, when they'd seen 'em,
They said, 'How to choose between 'em?
What one praises in its brother,
In the *other* one is for!'

Then she tried 'em with new make-up
On a sponsored run round Bacup,
And at Norwich for a porridge-
Eating contest which she won,

But, spilling 'em in Gillingham,
Her lobes felt light in Willingham,
And nothing else is filling 'em,
So now

The poem's

Done!

Mr Angelo

Mr Angelo's dead and gone,
And the worrying thought
Has entered my head:
How will the poor old man get on,
Him not speaking
A word of Dead?

Drinking Song

For weeks and weeks it wouldn't rain.
    My tree was growing rusty,
Leaves plugged with dust. Then suddenly
The rain came flooding like the sea.
The leaves went on a drinking spree.
I said, *How are you doing, tree?*
    My tree said, *Not so dusty!*

Zoob

I
am
ZOOB.

You can't fit me
in a triangle, a circle
or a cube.

I'm the empty seat beside you
on the 31 bus
or the Tube.

If you think you can describe me,
let me tell you that
you're making a
BOOB.

I can see round corners,
I can look in your eyes.
You can't see me,
but I'm wondrous wise.

I'm ZOOB.

That's whoob.

I'm what the wind means
when it moans,
'Zoob . . . Zoob.'

I'm what the sky says
when it groans,
'Zoob . . . Zoob.'

I'm as near as you are,
I'm as far as the sun,
I'm everything
And I am one:

I'm youb . . .

Zoob . . .

ZOOB . . .

ZOOB . . .

Fast Food

Dorothy Hogg had a hot-dog stand:
Hottest dogs in all the land.
East and south and north and west,
Dot Hogg's hot-dogs were the best!

What Was It?

What was it
that could make
me wake
in the middle of the night
when the light
was a long way from coming
and the humming
of the fridge was the single
tingle
of sound
all round?

Why, when I crept downstairs and watched
green numbers sprinting on the kitchen clock,
was I afraid the empty rocking chair
might start to rock?

Why, when I stole back up and heard
the creak of each stair to my own
heart's quickening beats,

was I afraid that I should find
some other thing from the night outside
between my sheets?

Mercy

Mercy her name was,
The blind lady.
Took her home from bingo
Each Wednesday night,
With her stick tap-rapping
On the breeze-blocks.
She'd humour and love.
No sight.

And suddenly
I recall
Salt of a tide of darkness
Swirling up under that door
She swam through with her key
And turned no light on.
Why should she?
She left all light
Behind her,
Needing none
To find things there:
Things, it seemed,
Could find her.

Mercy.
Took her home from bingo
Each Wednesday night,
With her stick tap-rapping
On the breeze-blocks.
Mercy.
Heart of light.

Dave Dirt's Christmas Presents

Dave Dirt wrapped his Christmas presents
Late on Christmas Eve
And gave his near relations things
That you would not believe.

His brother got an Odour-Eater –
Second-hand one, natch.
For Dad he chose, inside its box,
A single burnt-out match.

His sister copped the sweepings from
His hairy bedroom rug,
While Mum received a centipede
And Granny got a slug.

Next day he had the nerve to sit
Beneath the Christmas tree
And say: 'OK, I've done my bit –
What have you got for me?'

Irish Haiku

Animal mountains
Sleeping in each other's shade
In Connemara

Acorn Haiku

Just a green olive
In its own little egg-cup:
It can feed the sky.

The Head's Hideout

The Head crouched in his hideout
Beneath a dustbin lid.
'I want to see,' he muttered,
'No teacher and no kid,

No parent, no inspector,
Never a district nurse,
And, please, not one school dinner:
The things are getting worse!'

All morning, as the phone rang,
He hid away. Instead:
'The Head is in the dustbin,'
The secretary said.

'The *Head* is in the *dustbin*?'
'Yes, he'll be there all day.
He likes sometimes to manage
A little getaway.

Last year he went to Holland.
Next year he's off to France.
Today he's in the dustbin.
You have to take your chance.'

The Head sprang from the garbage
As end-of-school came round.
He cried, 'That's quite the nastiest
Hideaway I've found!

I think I'll stick to teachers
And kids and parents too.
It's just sometimes I've had enough.'
Don't blame him. Do you?

The Singing Spud

This is the story of Chinese Li,
Who lived with his mother in Liverpool 3.

She kept a shop and she sold fried fish
And chips as crisp as a person could wish,

So people said you'd have to be dippy
To go anywhere but Li's mum's chippy

For fish and chips or hot meat pies
Or pickled cukes of gigantic size.

Out in the back room all day long
Chinamen sat and they played mah-jong

With their faces turned into scowls or smiles
By the clackety-clack of the falling tiles.

And Li came back from school each day
And helped his mum in the following way:

He peeled the spuds and he poured them in
To a sort of tumbling mechanical bin,

A type of rumbling electrical barrow.
They went in round and they came out narrow.

The slicing machine! When you come to grips with it,
Start with spuds and you end with chips with it.

One day Li was churning them round
To that deep old, hungry, grumbling sound

When he was amazed to hear a song
Raised from the slicer, loud and long:

Oh, I am a spud, a very old spud,
And I do not wish to die.
I've missed the boat and I've lost my coat
But I do not care to lie
In a number of bits in a pan that spits –
Without ever knowing why.

So Li was quick as the flash of a fin.
He whisked that spud from the slicing tin

And he set it up on the chip-shop shelf
Where this ancient potato sat by itself.

And when the Chinamen came to play
Each one of them wished the spud good day:

'How are you doing? All right? OK?
Warm enough there? Good. That's the way!'

At night it was off for a roll downtown
On a piece of string that Li swung down.

Now, some keep dogs and some keep cats
And some have zebras and some have rats

But Li, by city wall and hedge,
Walked with nothing but a singing veg.:

> *Oh, I am a spud, a very old spud,*
> *And I'm glad I did not die.*
> *For I'm free to roll on an evening stroll,*
> *Which nobody can deny,*
> *And there's no spud in or out of mud*
> *That's quite as happy as I.*

It sings it once, then it sings it again.
Li's mum thinks the boy's insane!

Freeze

Pocked snow, cold-Christmas-pudding earth,
The tracery of winter trees,
The sky in danger with the dusk,
The mare's breath steaming in the freeze,

The sliding panes of river ice,
The olive water underneath,
The violet blade of last of light
That draws the darkness from its sheath.

Let's Hear it for the Limpet

If there's one animal that isn't a wimp, it
Is the limpet.

Let me provide an explanation
For my admiration.

To start with, it's got two thousand tiny teeth
Beneath

Its comical conical-hat-shaped, greeny-grey shell:
A tongue as well

That rasps the delicate seaweed through its front door:
What's more –

And this is what gives me the greatest surprise –
Two bright eyes

Indoors at the end of long tentacles poking out, which
Twitch.

But its funniest feature by far is its foot
That's put

Straight down to clamp it fast to the rock.
(Gulls knock,

You see, at the shell to try and winkle it off
For scoff.)

But the limpet does more with its foot than Ian Rush.
Forsaking the crush

Of its home life it stomps off, foraging, humping its
   shell with it,
Then thinks, 'The hell with it,'

And slithers back to exactly where it began.
What a man

Is the limpet, in his wilderness of weed!

Needless to say, they make very good pets indeed.

The Site

Lengths of scaffolding
Bonging like tuning forks,
Grumbling barrows
Rumbling out over the ramps,

Sun-tanned, shirtless workmen singing,
Pulley ropes from high windows swinging,
The bursts of a drill
That churns and chews and champs,

One day will be
Numbers 1, 2, 3,
Houses quiet as neighbours
In a sheet of stamps.

Something He Left

An overcoat warming a clothes-hanger,
Alone in a cupboard after his body had gone
To be made into flame and memory,
Standing as still as he placed it,
Or very faintly trembling,
The night before the dawn he put death on.

Dave Dirt Was on the 259

Dave Dirt was on the 259
(Down Seven Sisters Road it goes),
And since he'd nothing else to do
He stuck his ticket up his nose,

He shoved his pen-top in his ear,
He pulled three hairs out of his head,
He ate a page out of his book,
He held his breath till he went red,

He stuck his tongue out at the queue,
He found a nasty scab to pick,
He burped and blew a raspberry,
He imitated being sick,

He stuck a piece of bubblegum
Inside a dear old lady's bonnet.
If you should catch the 259,
Make sure that Dave Dirt isn't on it!

Frosty Winds Made Moan

Old Frosty Winds

Is grizzled and raddled and sozzled and saddled
With much unhappiness where he sits
On the bench in the shopping precinct
On winter afternoons.

Sometimes he shouts at the people
And sometimes he shouts at himself.

His beard is like broken glass and his clothes like
    garbage.
Poor Frosty Winds,

With only a bottle for company
And what he has to say
In the tearing weather
To his sad head.

Soon he'll be dead
As the litter that blows round his ankles,
As the supermarket tickets, screwed away, useless,
The bang of the trolleys that stack up alongside the
    wall
And the wind that will turn
On its journey.

What can you say to Frosty?
At least you can say goodbye.

Strange Service

A most peculiar postman
    is working down our street.
He doesn't *hand* the letters through –
    he does it with his feet.

A most unusual milkman
    is working in our town.
He swallows all the milk before
    he puts the bottles down.

A most uncommon dustman
    is working down our lane.
He takes the garbage round the back
    and throws it in again!

Objection

My feelings towards my little brother
Would soften
If only, once every so often,
He'd blow his nose.

He's not without style.
Why won't he, just once in a while,
Do you suppose?

As things are,
I just can't stick it.
Why can't he blow it
Instead of pick it?

Horace

The moon was a luminous toenail,
Far ingrown,
When poor old Horace the Hedgehog
Wandered alone,

Humping his heavy hackles
Over the lawn,
Weary as all the time
Before he was born,

Fearful of badgers and foxes
And human feet,
Looking for mice
To eat.

Poor old Horace the Hedgehog
Snuffled along,
Singing against the stars
His own sad song:

'Some might be glad to wear
A rug of prickles,
But, heavens, from the inside
How it tickles!'

Poor old Horace the Hedgehog
Shuffled away,
Singing his own sad song
Till his dying day:

'Some might like to be screwed up
Into a ball,
But it doesn't suit Horace –
It doesn't suit Horace

At all!'

Afternoon of a Prawn

I don't mind dawn.
Night comes and goes.
It's afternoon
Gets up my nose.

I wish I'd not
Been born a prawn.
I'd sooner be
A unicorn

Complete with horn,
But no such luck.
Wouldn't have minded
Being a duck –

At least I'd quack –
But all around
The salty seas
Prawns make no sound,

But a thin whistle,
A tedious song,
And afternoons
Grow far too long.

Nothing to do
With your see-through shell.
Afternoons
For prawns are hell.

I don't mind dawn.
Night comes and goes.
It's afternoons
Get up my nose.

Mirror Poem

If I look within the mirror,
Deep inside its frozen tears,
Shall I see the man I'll marry
Standing at my shoulder,
　　Leaning down the years?

Shall I smile upon the mirror,
Shall my love look, smiling, back?
Midnight on Midsummer's eve:
What becomes of marriage
　　If the glass should crack?

Finbar

flowers of frost
  bloom
    on the pane
  ice
in the arms
     of black trees
  glints
Finbar
  is born
  from his mother's
    womb
by forceps
     plucked
like
   winter
     fruit
        reach
his fingers
to the rising   sun
his heartbeat
   warms   the
   fro   zen
    day

Just Before Christmas

Down the Holloway Road on the top of the bus
On the just-before-Christmas nights we go,
Allie and me and all of us,
And we look at the lit-up shops below.
Orange and yellow the fruit stalls glow,
Store windows are sploshed with sort-of-snow,
And Santa's a poor old so-and-so,
With his sweating gear and his sack in tow,
And Christ . . . mas is coming!

At the front of the top of the lit-up bus
Way down the Holloway Road we ride,
Allie and me and all of us,
And the butchers chop and lop with pride,
And the turkeys squat with their stuffing inside
By ropes of sausages soon to be fried,
And every door is open wide
As down the road we growl or glide
And Christ . . . mas is coming!

All at the front of the top of the bus,
Far down the Holloway Road we roar,
Allie and me and all of us,
And tellies are tinselled in every store,
With fairy lights over every door,
With glitter and crêpe inside, what's more,
And everyone seeming to say, 'For sure,
Christmas is coming as never before.'
Yes, Christ . . . mas is coming!

The Moody Messenger

His walkie-talkie sneezes
And coughs as he goes by,
And something short and horrible
He spits out in reply.

He's a cross between a cowboy
And a moody astronaut,
Scowling from his fish bowl
(He's not the smiling sort).

He's among the meanest movers
Down any city street,
With a 1000-c.c. dragon
Snarling at hands and feet.

With a roar of rage he throttles.
The rubber grips and bites
And nearly knocks your knees off
When lunging from the lights.

He slouches into offices
And slams the package down.
Can you think of anything
To make him smile, not frown?

City Rain

After the storm
all night before
the world looked like
an upturned mop

wrung out into streets
half-dirty, half-clean,
tasting of rain
in bedraggled trees

and smelling of dog
with its shaky fur
and cold

lick.

Snarl

When Dave Dirt left the dentist,
He thought he'd better stop
And check out what the man had done.
He chose a darkened shop

He thought was shut for dinner.
He snarled in at the pane
To see his teeth reflected there
And then he snarled again.

But suddenly he noticed,
As he forced his lips out wide,
A cobbler staring at him who
Was mending shoes inside.

The cobbler looked quite horrified.
Dave looked as though he'd eat him.
He turned and ran off down the street.
Dave didn't want to meet him!

Applause

I gave my cat a six-minute standing ovation
For services rendered: hunting of very small game,

Pouncing about and sitting in cardboard boxes,
Three-legged washing and never knowing his name,

The jump on the knee, the nuzzle at night, the
    kneading
Of dough with his paws, the punch at the candle flame,

The yowling for food, the looking at everything
    otherwise,
Staring through it straight with a faraway aim.

I gave my cat a six-minute standing ovation.
Your cat's like that? I think you should do the same.

Dialogue between My Cat Bridget and Me

K: Can't you see
   I'm trying to write?
   Why jump on my knee?
   And why alight
   With muddy paws
   On verse brand-new?
   There should be laws
   Against cats like you.

B: *Can't you see*
   I'm writing too,
   Poems better
   Than you can do?

K: Is that a fact?
   We'll see about that.
   I must be cracked
   To put up with a cat
   That lies there dribbling
   And trying to bite a
   Bit off the ribbon
   Of my typewriter.

B: *I have to use*
   My tongue to say
   The words I want,
   Like you. OK?

K: Maybe so,
But I don't see how.
All you know
To speak's *miaow*.

B: Different *miaows*.
Sometimes I yell them,
Sometimes whisper:
It's the way I tell them.

K: You think you're a better
Poet than me?

B: *So* that's *what you're*
Supposed to be!

The Magic Box

I will put in the box

the swish of a silk sari on a summer night,
fire from the nostrils of a Chinese dragon,
the tip of a tongue touching a tooth.

I will put in the box

a snowman with a rumbling belly,
a sip of the bluest water from Lake Lucerne,
a leaping spark from an electric fish.

I will put in the box

three violet wishes spoken in Gujarati,
the last joke of an ancient uncle
and the first smile of a baby.

I will put in the box

a fifth season and a black sun,
a cowboy on a broomstick
and a witch on a white horse.

My box is fashioned from ice and gold and steel,
with stars on the lid and secrets in the corners.
Its hinges are the toe joints
of dinosaurs.

I shall surf in my box
on the great high-rolling breakers of the wild Atlantic,
then wash ashore on a yellow beach
the colour of the sun.